Kylie Jean

Cupcake Queen

by Marci Peschke

illustrated by Tuesday Mourning

PICTURE WINDOW BOOKS
a capstone imprint

Kylie Jean is published by Picture Window Books
A Capstone Imprint
1710 Roe Crest Drive
North Mankato, Minnesota 56003
www.capstoneyoungreaders.com

Library of Congress Cataloging-in-Publication Data
Peschke, M. (Marci)
  Cupcake queen / by Marci Peschke ; illustrated by Tuesday Mourning.
    p. cm. -- (Kylie Jean)
  Summary: Kylie Jean needs to find a way to make some spending money, and she decides that baking cupcakes for people--and dogs--and selling them at garage sales is the perfect solution.
  ISBN 978-1-4048-7580-7 (library binding) -- ISBN 978-1-4048-8102-0 (paper over board) -- ISBN 978-1-4795-1528-8 (ebook) -- ISBN 978-1-4795-6753-9 (paperback)
  1. Money-making projects for girls--Juvenile fiction. 2. Baking--Juvenile fiction. 3. Cupcakes--Juvenile fiction. 4. Garage sales--Juvenile fiction. 5. Dogs--Juvenile fiction. [1. Moneymaking projects--Fiction. 2. Baking--Fiction. 3. Cupcakes--Fiction. 4. Garage sales--Fiction. 5. Dogs--Fiction.] I. Mourning, Tuesday, ill. II. Title. III. Series: Peschke, M. (Marci) Kylie Jean.
  PZ7.P441245Cup 2013
  813.6--dc23   2012028531

Graphic Designer: Kristi Carlson
Editor: Beth Brezenoff
Production Specialist: Eric Manske

Design Element Credit:
Shutterstock/blue67design

Printed in China
092014
008472RRDS15

For Genny, the Real True Cupcake Queen
—MP

Table of Contents

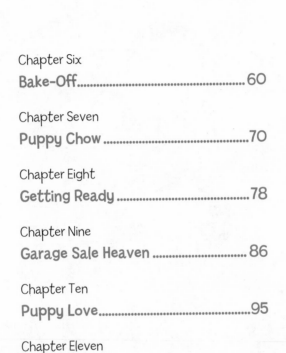

All About Me, Kylie Jean!

My name is Kylie Jean Carter. I live in a big, sunny, yellow house on Peachtree Lane in Jacksonville, Texas with Momma, Daddy, and my two brothers, T.J. and Ugly Brother.

T.J. is my older brother, and Ugly Brother is . . . well . . . he's really a dog. Don't you go telling him he is a dog. Okay? I mean it. He thinks he is a real true person.

He is a black-and-white bulldog. His front looks like his back, all smashed in. His face is all droopy like he's sad, but he's not.

His two front teeth stick out, and his tongue hangs down. (Now you know why his name is Ugly Brother.)

Everyone I love to the moon and back lives in Jacksonville. Nanny, Pa, Granny, Pappy, my aunts, my uncles, and my cousins all live here. I'm extra lucky, because I can see all of them any time I want to!

My momma says I'm pretty. She says I have eyes as blue as the summer sky and a smile as sweet as an angel. (Momma says pretty is as pretty does. That means being nice to the old folks, taking care of little animals, and respecting my momma and daddy.)

But I'm pretty on the outside and on the inside. My hair is long, brown, and curly.

I wear it in a ponytail sometimes, but my absolute most favorite is when Momma pulls it back in a princess style on special days.

I just gave you a little hint about my big dream. Ever since I was a bitty baby I have wanted to be an honest-to-goodness beauty queen. I even know the wave. It's side to side, nice and slow, with a dazzling smile. I practice all the time, because everybody knows beauty queens need to have a perfect wave.

I'm Kylie Jean, and I'm going to be a beauty queen. Just you wait and see!

Chapter One
Saturday Sales

On Saturday mornings, my favorite thing to do is go to garage sales! As soon as I wake up, I get excited. Today I get to go with Momma, Granny, and Pappy. I love garage sales!

I look out my window and notice that the sky is streaked with gray, gold, and pink. Then I notice something else. Granny and Pappy are already parked in front of our house on Peachtree Lane, waiting for me and Momma. I bet Pa's rooster hasn't even crowed yet.

I better hurry up! If I take too long, Pappy will honk the horn and wake up Miss Clarabelle, my neighbor.

I hurry to get dressed. Momma calls, "Kylie Jean, are you ready to go yet?"

"Almost," I yell. "Don't leave without me. Okay?"

I just need my pink purse. It's not anywhere in my room. When I go downstairs, Ugly Brother is waiting by the front door.

I ask, "Did you see my purse?"

He barks, "Ruff."

One bark means no.

If I have to go to the sales without any money, it won't be much fun.

"Come on, Kylie Jean," Momma calls from the kitchen. "Granny and Pappy are waiting."

"Ugly Brother, please, please help me look for it!" I beg.

Then I see something pink poking out from under his tail, so I run over and pull out my purse. It has a sparkly cupcake on the front.

"Ugly Brother!" I yell. "Were you lying to me?"

He whines and lies down on the floor. He looks sad. Then I realize why he hid my purse.

"You don't want me to leave, do you, boy," I say, giving him a pat.

Ugly Brother agrees. "Ruff, ruff!"

I grab my purse. When I shake it, I can tell there's money inside, so I don't need to go back to my room and get money from my piggy bank. A girl has to have money to go shopping, right?

"Ready, Momma!" I say. She walks into the living room and we head outside.

Momma slides across the giant back seat of Pappy's old-timey car. I scoot in beside her.

Momma announces, "Sorry, everybody. We're running late because Kylie Jean lost her purse again."

Pappy laughs. "It always takes that pretty little girl a while to get ready," he says. "I was getting ready to honk, but then you came on out."

Granny asks, "Who's hungry for pancakes?"

"I'm so hungry for pancakes I could eat a full stack all by myself!" I say.

Pappy smiles. "Okay, first pancakes, then garage sales," he says.

Before I know it, we're pulling in to the Pancake Palace. It's a funny building that looks like a castle. Outside, it is covered with stone. It has heavy wood doors and a tower with a tiny window. Inside, the floor is red and white like a checkerboard, and the tables are red, too.

We sit down. Our waitress comes to take our order right away. "How are y'all?" she asks. "What are you having today? Coffee, right?"

I say, "We're peachy keen, and today I'm a garage sale queen. I would like a short stack and juice, please, ma'am."

Momma, Pappy, and Granny all order their breakfasts. Our waitress scratches it all down on a notepad with her pencil, and then disappears into the kitchen. Faster than you can say "flapjacks," she comes back with a tray loaded down with our food.

My plate is piled high with pancakes. I pour syrup all over the top of my pancakes, and it runs down over the edge of the plate and onto the table.

"Oops!" I exclaim.

Momma dips her napkin in her water glass and hands it to me. She says, "Wipe up that mess right away, Kylie Jean, or you'll be too sticky to go to garage sales."

It's quiet while we eat. We are all too busy chewing to do much talking!

Once Pappy and I are done eating, he leans over and whispers, "If you're going to garage sales, you gotta have a plan." Then he shows me the sale ads in the paper.

Using a pink marker, we circle the ones that say "huge" or "big sale." Sometimes more than one family or even a group like a church will have a sale. You have to know the best neighborhoods for sales, too. Some places only have junk, and you want to find the really good stuff.

We map out our route and load into the car. We are ready to shop, shop, shop!

At the first sale, Momma gets a fancy new dress with the tags still on it for five dollars.

While she pays, I notice that there's a boy selling ice-cold water in bottles for one dollar each. It is already hot out, so lots of people are buying water while they wait to pay.

In the car, Momma says, "Wasn't that little boy selling water cute?"

"He was a born salesman," Granny says. "He asked everyone who walked up to buy water."

The next sale is on River Road.

Granny digs through a box of junky jewelry and buys an old necklace for fifty cents. After she pays, Granny puts the necklace in the palm of my hand. I like the sparkly fake diamonds on it. They twinkle like stars in a night sky.

As we leave, I see that at this sale, there's a boy sitting behind a card table. He's selling some watery pink Kool-Aid for fifty cents a cup. His pitcher has flies buzzing around it. Ick! Flies remind me of Pa's cow pasture.

On Dogwood Street, Pappy buys an old camera for two dollars. A little bitty girl and her big sister are out front selling lemonade for twenty-five cents.

Granny tells the girls, "You sure do have a good price on your lemonade. I'll take a cup."

The sister helps the tiny girl pour Granny a cup. We head to the car.

Granny takes a sip and makes a terrible scrunched-up face. She cries, "They forgot to put the sugar in this! It's so sour, it will curl your hair."

The last sale we go to is at my friend Cara's house. I find the cutest orange stuffed kitten for a dollar.

I show the little kitty to Momma. "Isn't this little cat adorable?" I ask.

Momma doesn't say anything because she does not want me to have any more stuffed animals. I count out all of my change and Cara helps me count, too. I only have sixty-eight cents.

"Please, Momma, can I borrow some money?" I ask sweetly. "I just need a little bit more. I can pay you back when we get home."

Momma shakes her head. "No way, little lady," she says. "You have too many stuffed toys already!"

Pappy says, "I'll lend you the money. If you'll make me a promise."

"Okay," I say. "I'll do anything for this cute little kitten!"

Pappy looks me in the eye and asks, "Do you promise to give away one of your stuffed animals to your cousin Lucy?"

Right away, I agree. "Yup! I promise." Then he grins and gives me a loan.

Borrowing money is not easy. I think I better get my very own job. Then I can buy any ol' thing I want!

As we are leaving, I see sodas in a cooler full of ice. There's a sign that says, "Cokes for $1.50 each."

Cara asks, "Do you want to buy some Cokes?"

"They sure do look icy cold, sweet, and delicious!" I say, glancing at Pappy.

"We'll take four of those drinks," Pappy says, handing Cara six dollars. "Here you go!"

Cara is getting RICH! And she's not the only one. At almost every sale there has been a kid out front selling something! I need to get a business, too!

Chapter Two
Teatime Treats

On Sunday, we go to church, but we don't go to Lickskillet Farm for Sunday dinner afterward. Instead, we're going to a tea party at Miss Clarabelle's! Lucy gets to come, too.

Miss Clarabelle sent us a fancy invitation and everything. The invitation had pink roses on it and smelled like roses, too. We had to R.S.V.P., which means telling her if we are coming or not.

On the way home from church, Lucy and I sit all the way in the back of the van so we can have a little chat. T.J. sits in the middle. Daddy and Momma sit in the front.

I ask Lucy, "Did you know kids can get rich?"

"I never thought about it much," she says. "How do they do it?"

T.J. turns around and says, "They probably have to get a real job like me."

"They were not mowing lawns," I say. "They were selling stuff to drink at garage sales."

I explain all about the water, Kool-Aid, lemonade, and sodas.

"So that's how I figured out I need to start a business," I tell Lucy.

"What kind of drinks are you going to sell?" she asks.

I shake my head. "I like to be different, so I don't want to sell stuff to drink," I explain.

Lucy raises an eyebrow. She says, "We have all afternoon to think of something."

I know she's right. Pa always says that two heads are better than one.

When we pull in to our driveway, Ugly Brother is sitting right in the middle of it waiting for us. I think he would like to go with us on Sundays, but Momma says dogs do not belong in church.

As we climb out of the van, Momma warns us, "You girls, don't go gettin' all dirty before your tea party."

We say, "Yes, ma'am!"

We can hardly wait until two o'clock for teatime. But we have things to do before the party. First we all sit down at the kitchen table for some leftover fried chicken and potato salad for lunch.

When we're done eating, I ask, "Is it time yet?"

Momma says, "No. Run along and play. I'll call you when it's time."

Lucy, Ugly Brother, and I go upstairs so Lucy can pick out one of my stuffed animals to take home. I promised Pappy I would give her one, and I always keep my promises.

In my room, Lucy looks at dogs, bunnies, kittens, bears, an elephant, and a pink pony. She says, "I sure do like this pony, but you probably want to keep it."

She keeps on looking. Finally she finds a cute little turtle. "Can I have this one?" she asks.

"Yup!" I say.

We play for a while. Then we hear Momma holler that it's time for tea. We jump up, fluffing out the skirts of our church dresses. My dress is pink with white trim and fluffy sleeves. I'm going to wear my little white gloves, too. Lucy has on a polka-dot dress.

Downstairs, Ugly Brother also wants to go to the tea party, but he is not invited. Momma says bringing an extra guest is rude. Poor Ugly Brother! He has been stuck at home all day!

Lucy and I cross Miss Clarabelle's yard, being extra careful not step on her pretty flowers.

On the porch, there is a fancy iron table set with a polka-dot tablecloth. On top of the table there's a sparkly glass vase full of pink roses.

I say, "I bet those roses are from Miss Clarabelle's garden."

When we get closer, I can see the teapot with little pink flowers on it and the little teacups.

"Ooh la la!" Lucy whispers. "This is a fancy party."

I ring the doorbell. Miss Clarabelle comes to the door carrying a silver tray.

"Well, good afternoon, young ladies," she says. "I am so glad you could come for tea."

"Good afternoon," Lucy whispers.

I add, "Thank you for inviting us."

Miss Clarabelle asks, "Can one of you hold the door, please?"

I swing the door open and Miss Clarabelle puts the tray on the table. We follow her. She says, "Please have a seat and I will be right back."

The tray has teeny tiny cucumber and chicken salad tea sandwiches. Yum!

There is also a plate of juicy red strawberries and glistening green grapes.

Lucy says, "Everything looks so tasty."

I agree, "Yup."

Then we don't talk much. And that's weird for me and Lucy. Usually we're talking all the time! That tells you this tea is real special.

When Miss Clarabelle joins us, she's carrying a little silver stand with cookies shaped like teapots and tiny pink cupcakes. She notices my white gloves and says, "Kylie Jean, ladies remove their gloves for tea."

I slip my gloves off as Miss Clarabelle sits down. Then I ask, "Ma'am, are there other rules for having tea?"

Miss Clarabelle says, "Oh my, yes! Would you like to learn about them?"

"Yes, ma'am!" we exclaim.

She tells us all about the tea rules.

Tea Etiquette

1. Ladies always remove their gloves before enjoying tea.

2. Ladies put their napkins in their laps.

3. The hostess always pours tea once the guests are seated.

4. Ladies stir their tea gently, careful not to tap the sides of the cup.

5. Ladies do not stick out their pinky fingers while drinking tea.

Now that we know our tea manners, we are
ready for tea.

First we put milk and sugar in our teacups. Miss
Clarabelle pours the tea from her momma's china
teapot. She is careful not to fill our cups too full.
Then she looks at me and says, "Please pass the
tea sandwiches."

The silver tray is heavy, but
I do my best. She puts two tea
sandwiches on her plate.
Lucy and I do the same.
Then we pass the sweets
around.

I ask, "May I please have two cookies?"

Miss Clarabelle replies, "Yes, since you asked so
nicely."

Lucy asks, "Then may I please have two cookies, too?"

Miss Clarabelle smiles and agrees. We each add a cupcake to our plate and then it's finally time to eat.

Lucy takes a big bite of her cookie and mumbles, "This cookie is scrumptious."

I remind her, "Momma says don't talk with your mouth full."

Lucy swallows and says, "Sorry." I smile at her so she won't feel embarrassed.

We keep eating our delightful treats. My favorite things are the strawberry cream cupcakes. The frosting is so sweet and creamy. They are just delicious!

"It's nice of you to come to tea," Miss Clarabelle says. "Sometimes I get so lonely in this old house."

We smile. "Thanks for inviting us," I say. "Tea parties are fun!"

"What have you girls been doing lately?" Miss Clarabelle asks.

I explain all about my plan to start a business.

"What a wonderful idea!" Miss Clarabelle says. "It's important for young women to learn about business."

Lucy says, "Now she just has to think of something to sell."

Just then, an idea hits me faster than buttercream frosting on red velvet cake! I'm going to sell cupcakes!

Chapter Three
In Business

I can't wait to tell Momma and Ugly Brother all about my plan to sell cupcakes!

After we're done with our tea party, Lucy and I thank Miss Clarabelle for inviting us. Then we skip all the way across the yard.

At my house, Aunt Susie is already here to pick up Lucy. She and Momma are having coffee in the kitchen.

As we walk in, Aunt Susie says, "Well, don't you girls look sweeter than sugar."

Momma laughs and says, "They're probably full of sugar! Miss Clarabelle is a fabulous baker."

"Did you girls have fun?" Aunt Susie asks. "How was tea?"

We tell them all about the sandwiches, teapot cookies, and yummy cupcakes. Momma looks at Aunt Susie and says, "I think we should have had tea instead of coffee. Those treats sound delicious!"

"Tea is better than coffee," I say.

"Especially with lots of milk and sugar!" Lucy adds, giggling.

After they leave, I tell Momma all about my plan. When I'm done talking, Momma thinks for a minute. Then she says, "Kylie Jean, I love the idea of you starting a business. But you'll need to invest your own money in it."

"What does that mean?" I ask nervously. I don't have very much money.

"That means you'll use your allowance to buy ingredients," Momma explains.

Ugly Brother and I run upstairs to dump my piggy bank and count the change.

There are lots of quarters, dimes, and pennies, and some paper money. I count all the coins, stacking them up into little piles. I put four quarters in each stack so they are each worth a dollar.

Ugly Brother tries to sniff the stacks.

"No, Ugly Brother!" I shout. "You better let me count them before you knock them over."

He barks, "Ruff, ruff."

There are ten one-dollar bills, a five-dollar bill, and a ten-dollar bill. With all of my coins, I have thirty dollars.

Wow! I'm already rich!

Looking at all my money, I realize I've been saving it for something special, and this is it! And once I make more money, I can buy anything I want when I go shopping.

I run downstairs to tell Momma. She's in the kitchen, talking to T.J.

"I have thirty dollars!" I shout.

T.J. asks, "Can I borrow some money?"

"No way!" I say. "I need all my money to buy the ingredients for my cupcake business."

"You should make chocolate cupcakes," T.J. says.

"Hmm," I say. "Momma, what kind do you think I should make?"

Momma thinks for a minute. "My favorite is red velvet with cream cheese frosting," she says. "But Daddy's favorite is lemon. And I know you like vanilla best, right?"

"That's right," I say.

I think about it a little bit more. "I also like strawberry, because they're pink," I add. "If I make everybody's favorite, I could have four flavors. Or should I do more?"

"Four flavors is plenty," Momma tells me.

"Where are you going to sell your cupcakes?" T.J. asks.

My mouth falls open. Oh no! My plan to start my own business will fall apart unless someone has a garage sale!

Chapter Four
Hello, Cupcake!

The next afternoon, I am busy making myself
an after-school snack when Daddy comes into the
kitchen. He says, "Hello, cupcake!"

Grinning, I say, "Hello, Daddy!" Before he can
say anything else, I decide to tell him about my
problem. "I need someone to have a garage sale so
I can sell my cupcakes. Can you pretty please have
one? Oh, and can it be this Saturday?"

Daddy laughs. "That's not much time to get
ready for a big sale."

"I can help get everything ready," I say. "Ugly Brother can help, too!"

Ugly Brother whines and puts his paws over his head. I lower my voice and tell him, "I think you are starting to be a big ol' lazy bones!" When he hears me say "bones," he barks. I'm not sure if he is barking because he is lazy or hungry.

Daddy looks at me. "Let's talk to your momma over dinner and see what she thinks," he suggests. "Okay, cupcake?"

I nod. "Yes, sir."

We are having spaghetti and meatballs for dinner. Ugly Brother only likes the meatballs, because the noodles stick to his tongue. That makes them hard for him to eat.

Momma lets me put the silverware on the table and fold the napkins. When I'm done, she hugs me and says, "This table looks amazing!"

T.J. comes in, sniffing the air. "And somethin' smells amazin'!" he says. "What's for dinner?"

I tell him, "Spaghetti and meatballs, bread, and salad. Yummy!"

We all take our seats around the big table. Daddy says grace and we dig in.

T.J. loads up. He has a little mountain of pasta noodles and meatballs on his plate. Momma passes the salad and bread.

Everything is delicious.

We are so busy eating that I almost forget to bring up the big garage sale!

Luckily, Daddy remembers.

"Why don't we have a big garage sale this weekend?" he asks Momma. "The weather is going to be just right."

Momma raises an eyebrow. "I'm sure Kylie Jean put you up to this so she can sell cupcakes," she begins. Then she sighs and says, "But that garage needs a good cleanin', so I say let's do it."

"Yay!" I shout. Ugly Brother and T.J. both groan.

After dinner, we spend all evening cleaning out the garage! I'm getting tired and there are a lot of skeeters out, but the garage is full of junky treasure.

First we push all the boxes to one side of the garage. Then we start opening them to see what's inside. It's fun, like a real treasure hunt!

Momma finds a box of old baby stuff. It has sippy cups, bottles, baby toys, blankets, and clothes.

"Were those things mine or T.J.'s?" I ask.

Momma says, "They're all pink, so they must have been yours."

"Aww," I say, looking at a teeny tiny dress. "I was such an itty bitty baby."

"You sure were," Momma says. "And some other momma will love to buy these sweet clothes and other baby things for her little girl."

Daddy and T.J. find a big box of old coins and stamps. When he was a little kid, T.J. collected that kind of stuff.

Daddy thinks someone will buy them. He finds some tools to sell, too. We're finding lots of things to sell!

Piles of stuff are everywhere. I can't even see Ugly Brother.

I call him and he barks, wiggling out of a pile of coats.

Momma is sorting and organizing the piles. One big pile is just trash.

Daddy starts loading all of the trash into the back of his truck to take to the city dump, and T.J. helps him.

"You and Ugly Brother could go to your room and pick out some of your old toys to sell at the garage sale," Momma tells me. "You can keep the money from any of your toys that sell."

"Okay," I shout, clapping my hands. Ugly Brother and I run to my room. Well, I run. Ugly Brother doesn't.

Choosing toys to sell turns out to be a lot harder than I thought it would be! I pick out some dollies, but I want to keep them all. I lay all them on my bed and look at them. I finally decide to sell my lemon cupcake cutie doll.

Ugly Brother brings me a purple stuffed bear.

"Okay, we can sell that bear," I agree. "What other animals can we sell? Not my pony. Okay, Ugly Brother?"

Ugly Brother barks, "Ruff, ruff." Then he brings me a rainbow fish, a little gray mouse, a pink kitty, and a green frog. I don't really want to sell them, but I put them in the pile anyway.

Ugly Brother helps me put them all in a box, and we take them down to the garage.

When Momma looks in the box, she exclaims, "I am so proud of you for choosin' some toys to sell in the sale. Good job!"

I say, "Thank you, Momma."

Momma checks her watch. "You have to go to school tomorrow," she says. "It's bedtime."

While I get ready for bed, I think about all of the great stuff we found to sell.

After I climb up in the bed and pull the covers all around me, Ugly Brother jumps up and scoots up right beside me so we are snug as two bugs in a rug.

I fall asleep petting his ear.

All night long, I dream about making cupcakes. I bake them and frost them with fluffy white icing. They are not plain old cupcakes. Instead, I put little doggie bone treats on the top. Ugly Brother eats them up!

When I wake up, I have a new idea! I'm not just gonna make cupcakes for people. My business will sell cupcakes for dogs, too!

Chapter Five
Cupcake Queen

When I get to school, I go straight to my classroom and sit down at the table I share with Cara, Paula, and Lucy.

I can't wait to tell Paula and Cara about my cupcake plan. Lucy already knows all about it, except for the doggie cupcake part.

I announce, "I am going into the bakery business and sellin' cupcakes! All kinds of cupcakes — even some for doggies!"

The girls gush, "Ohhh!"

"You must be so excited," Cara says.

"Yup," I say, adding, "I'm startin' my own business so I can get rich! Momma and I are startin' the bakin' tonight."

Paula looks puzzled. "You know dogs don't buy cupcakes, right?" she says. "Are your cupcakes going to be free? Because sellin' things to dogs is a bad plan if you're trying to get rich."

"No, silly," I say. "The people who own the dogs will buy the cupcakes."

"Oh," she says. "I get it." But she doesn't look too sure.

All morning, it seems like the clock is stuck! The time passes by slower than the roller coaster line at the state fair.

When the clock finally says eleven, it is time for lunch. Usually we bring our lunch, but today they are having corn dogs. Nothing tastes better for lunch than a nice hot corn dog covered in ketchup.

The lunch room is big and has rows and rows of brightly colored round tables. It's so noisy! You have to yell or no one can hear you.

While my friends and I wait in line, I see some kids with Popsicles on their tray. Pointing, I shout, "Hey, it's lucky Popsicle tray day."

Lucky Popsicle tray day is amazing! Some kids who buy their lunches get FREE Popsicles on their trays. I just know Lucy will get one. She is luckier than a four-leaf clover.

Sure enough, she gets a pink one. Well, you know pink is my color and I have the best cousin in the whole wide world because she wants to give her Popsicle to me.

Lucy hands it over, saying, "You take it, Kylie Jean. Look, it's your favorite flavor — pink lemonade."

I am so excited about my cupcakes I can't even eat it, so I say, "No thanks, Lucy," and give it back. Lucy stuffs the Popsicle into her mouth before she eats her corn dog and fries.

I laugh, and she smiles at me with her pink Popsicle mouth.

Normally I just love recess, but today even recess takes a long, long time. I can't wait to test out cupcake recipes with Momma. I just know they'll come out de-li-cious!

Momma is a blue-ribbon baker. Every year she wins prizes at the fair. Besides, just the way folks eat up her good food tells you she is the best cook in the county. Maybe even the whole state of Texas! She is gonna help me make the best cupcakes ever.

When we get back to our classroom, the rest of the day goes by slower than molasses in January. Finally, the last bell rings!

I grab my backpack and head for the door. It seems like the whole class is in line in front of me and they're all taking forever.

From the back of the line, I shout, "If y'all don't hurry up, some of us are going to miss our bus!" My complaining doesn't seem to rush them very much. Everyone likes to take their sweet time. They must not have cupcakes to bake.

We push through the crowded hallway and out the double doors into the sunshine. My bus is at the front of the line today. Yay for Mr. Jim! He is our bus driver. If he were a cupcake, he'd be chocolate cake because he has dark brown hair.

Jumping on the bus, I shout, "Hurry, Mr. Jim! Drive as fast as you can."

"Whoa, slow down," he says, wiping his face with his red bandana. "What's your big hurry anyway, gal?"

I explain, "Momma has an apron waiting for me and I need to get busy quick so I can sell a million cupcakes and be a cupcake queen!"

Mr. Jim looks surprised. I surprise him a lot, I think.

I slide into the seat right behind him and get busy doing my math problems. Usually I have a little chat with Mr. Jim, but not today.

I don't even ask him any math questions!

By the time we pick up the middle school kids, I am done with math and moving on to my spelling list. Right after we pick up T.J. and the high school kids, I finish all my homework.

Stuffing my book in my backpack, I shout, "Done!" Mr. Jim gives me a thumbs-up.

Soon we pull up in front of our house. As I get off the bus, I ask, "How many cupcakes do you want to buy, Mr. Jim?"

He says, "I might just have to buy a whole dozen. You're going to need to sell a lot of cupcakes to get to a million!"

Chapter Six
Bake-Off

Momma is in the kitchen getting ready to bake. She is wearing an apron with little pink and brown cupcakes all over the material.

I gush, "Oh, Momma, I just love your new apron!"

Momma smiles. "Turn around and close your eyes," she says. "I have something for you."

Momma slips an apron over my head. Then she ties it on with a big bow.

"Open your eyes," she says.

The apron looks just like Momma's. I smooth the front and whisper, "I love it! Where did you get it?"

"I told Granny about your new business," Momma says. "She made them for us. Now, let's get started!"

Cupcake recipes are laid out in neat rows on the kitchen table. Momma and I sit down to decide which ones to make.

It is a hard decision. Everyone likes chocolate and vanilla. Momma's favorite is red velvet. Strawberry and Italian cream cake are both good, too.

And I definitely want to make a special recipe Momma found for doggie cupcakes!

I ask, "How are we going to choose flavors?"

"You should make chocolate and vanilla, plus the dog recipe. Then choose two other flavors for variety," Momma suggests.

I choose strawberry because I like the pink frosting. Then I pick red velvet since most folks like it. I put the recipe cards next to the big bowl mixer.

"Which one is first?" I ask.

"Let's start with the chocolate," Momma decides.

We read the recipe carefully. Momma calls out the ingredients and I fetch them for her.

She lists, "Flour, sugar, butter, eggs, milk, cocoa, salt, baking powder, and vanilla."

I gather them up and tote them over to Momma.

First, we beat the golden butter until it is fluffy. I measure in the sugar as the mixer buzzes along.

Next comes the tricky part — cracking the eggs. Momma hands me a little bowl. Standing at the kitchen table, I tap the egg on the side of the bowl, watching a crack break across its middle. Pressing the sides of the egg, I hold my breath. I don't want the shell to break into the bowl along with the egg.

"Oh no!" I cry as I see little pieces of shell swirling in the egg.

Momma winks. "Try again, sweetie. It takes practice."

The bowl gets a rinse in the sink and I get another egg. This time the egg slides right out into the bowl with no shell. Yay!

But the recipe calls for two eggs. Can I do it again? Momma hands me another egg. I tap the egg, and success! It slips into the bowl, no shell. Momma adds them to the big mixing bowl. The beaters go buzz, buzz. The vanilla smells sweet when I carefully pour it into a measuring spoon.

I add flour and cocoa. The beaters are coated with fudgy goodness. It's starting to look pretty tasty, but we are too busy to try any.

Momma asks, "Can you put the cupcake liners in the pans?"

"Yes, ma'am," I say.

The cupcake liners stick together. I gently pull them apart and sort out the pink ones. Momma scoops the chocolate batter into the pretty pink paper cupcake liners, careful not to get any on the ruffled edges. Before you know it, that batch is in the oven and the kitchen smells yummy.

Time for a new batch! We rinse, wipe, wash, and get everything ready to start again.

The back door slams as T.J. comes in. "Where's my cupcake?" he asks.

"Sorry, these cupcakes are for my business," I tell him.

Then an idea hits me like candles on birthday cake! "If you want to earn a cupcake," I say, "you could do some work for me. I could pay you in cupcakes!"

T.J. laughs. "What do I have to do?" he asks.

"That's easy," I say. "Help us make cupcakes!"

T.J. always tries to make everything a contest. He says, "Let's have a bake-off to see who makes the best cupcakes!"

I make the strawberry, with light pink icing. Momma helps me a little, but she mostly makes her red velvet cupcakes, bakes the doggie cupcakes, and ices the chocolate cupcakes with red icing. T.J. makes vanilla, and a big mess! He has so much flour on him that he looks like a polar bear.

I put a doggie treat on top of one of the doggie cupcakes. "Why did you do that?" T.J. asks. "Nobody wants to eat a cupcake with a dog treat on it!"

"Dogs do!" I say. "I'm selling doggie cupcakes."

T.J. thinks about it for a minute. "You know, that's a pretty good idea," he says.

"I know!" I say proudly.

When Daddy comes home, we're still busy baking. He says, "This kitchen smells sweeter than a candy factory."

T.J. nods. "We're having a baking contest," he explains, "and you get to be the judge."

"Lucky me!" Daddy laughs. "Can Ugly Brother judge the ones with the dog bones on top?"

We all look at Ugly Brother. His tongue is hanging out of his mouth.

"I think he's counting on it," Momma says.

Ugly Brother is so excited about getting a cupcake that he chases his tail in a circle. Momma pours Daddy a tall glass of milk. She brings it to the table. Then I set three cupcakes on a pretty blue plate and carry them to Daddy.

I set the dog bone cupcake on the floor. Ugly Brother gobbles it up and barks, "Ruff, ruff!"

Daddy takes a big bite of each cupcake. Ugly Brother whines under the table.

Daddy says, "The winner is . . ."

You probably already guessed. Momma wins the bake-off!

Chapter Seven
Puppy Chow

The vanilla doggie bone cupcakes look good, and Ugly Brother has tried several. He loves them, but he eats anything. I wonder if other dogs will like them, too.

"Do you think other doggies will like my cupcakes?" I ask.

He barks, "Ruff."

One bark means no, but I do not believe him. He just wants to eat all the cupcakes.

Before I sell any cupcakes, I have to make sure other dogs will like them. Suddenly, an idea hits me like fleas on a dog. The Puppy Place Doggie Shelter is the perfect spot to bring cupcakes and find out if other doggies will like them.

So the next day after school, that's what my plan is! On the way home on the bus, I tell Mr. Jim all about my business.

"Have you ever heard of cupcakes for dogs?" I ask as soon as I get on the bus.

"No, can't say that I have," he replies.

"That's because I made them up," I tell him. "Ugly Brother loves them. Today I'm going to try them out on some other dogs."

"I'm a cat person," he mutters.

I pat his arm and smile. "It's okay if you like cats better," I say. What I don't tell him is that he gave me a great idea about cat cupcakes for later!

When I get off the bus, I wave to Mr. Jim with my beauty queen wave, nice and slow, side to side. He waves back.

Inside, Momma makes me change clothes. Once I pull on shorts and a T-shirt, I am ready to pack up a bag full of cupcakes. But as I'm riding my bike over to the shelter, I notice that Ugly Brother is tagging along.

"Just because you're comin' doesn't mean you can have another cupcake," I tell him. He whines, but keeps right on following me.

The Puppy Place is in an old mossy green house on River Street, down from the library.

The man who works at the shelter is Mr. Jay. His beard is gold like a lion, and he has a big laugh.

"Hi, Mr. Jay," I say. "I was wonderin' if it would be okay to give the doggies a treat today."

"What kind of treat, little miss?" he asks.

I explain all about my doggie cupcakes, and Mr. Jay smiles. "The pups will love getting a special treat," he says. "Follow me."

Ugly Brother and I follow him into the back of the house, where there is one big room with neat rows of cages along the walls. Right away, I notice the cutest little girl doggie named Countess. She is black and has a wrinkly face. I run over to get a closer look at her. She licks my hand.

"She's a sweetheart," Mr. Jay says. "I like to call her Tess."

I ask, "Can Tess come out of her cage to play with Ugly Brother?"

Mr. Jay lets her out. First Ugly Brother and Tess sniff each other a lot. Then they start playing with a pink chew toy.

While they play, Mr. Jay and I pass out cupcakes to all the sweet little doggies. The puppies love them. There's a wiener dog, a poodle, a lab, and a terrier.

"What kind of dog is Tess?" I ask.

"She is a Shar-Pei," Mr. Jay tells me. Then he sighs and adds, "I hate to do it, but I am going to have to close the Puppy Palace. I don't have enough money to keep it open."

I gasp. "Oh no! I hope all of these doggies get new homes soon!"

"They'll have to," Mr. Jay says. "I'm going to close in one week."

Ugly Brother puts his paws over his eyes and whines. This is terrible news. There has to be a way we can help.

Poor Ugly Brother hates to leave his new friend, but we promised to be back by dinnertime. Besides, I need to talk to Momma and Daddy about something important!

On the way home, I think about finding homes for all of those doggies. We could probably make sure the doggies there find new places to live, but if Mr. Jay closes, what happens if more dogs need help?

Slamming the door, I shout, "I need help!"

Everyone comes running. Momma asks, "Are you okay?"

"They are closing Puppy Place!" I cry. "We have to help Mr. Jay get enough money to stay open."

"Let's give the shelter our garage sale money," T.J. suggests.

"That's a great idea, son," Daddy says. "And my newspaper can run a story about the Puppy Place. Maybe it will get folks to donate."

I can't wait to tell Mr. Jay. I call him right up to say Daddy is going to put the shelter in the paper. He is so happy he hardly can talk. That's okay. I'm pretty good at talking, so I tell him all about our garage sale, too.

Mr. Jay is quiet for a minute after I tell him. Then he says, "You really do love dogs. Keeping the shelter open will save a lot of pups. They can't say thank you, but I am very grateful for any help your family can give us."

"Don't worry. Everything is going to be just fine. Goodbye for now," I tell him as I hang up.

Now it's really important for our sale to make a lot of money. Tomorrow when we get ready, we'll have to put higher prices on our old stuff. I sure hope folks will buy it all up.

Chapter Eight
Getting Ready

On Friday, I ask Cara, Paula, and Lucy to come home with me after school. My family is going to need help getting ready for the big sale. Our teacher lets us go to the office and use the phone during recess so they can get permission to ride the bus with me.

When Mr. Jim sees us all waiting at the bus door, he frowns and says, "Hold on just a minute! I see one girl who rides this bus and three who don't."

I smile my best dazzling beauty queen smile. Then I explain all about the dog shelter, the sale, and how we went to the office to use the phone. I can tell he wants me to finish talking, because his mouth is open like he wants to say something.

"Are you sayin' you have a note from the office that gives these girls permission to ride my bus today?" Mr. Jim says once I quit talking.

"Yes!" I say, throwing my hands up. "That's what I've been sayin'!"

By now there is a big long line behind us so we jump on the bus. I sit with Lucy. Cara and Paula sit across from us. We can't wait to get busy working. Before long, we pull up in front of my house. I see Daddy's truck in the driveway. He's home early to help, too!

Momma and Daddy are in the garage sorting things. Momma is the boss. She smiles when she sees us.

"Girls, you can make the signs and put the price tag stickers on things," she says. "T.J., bring out all those clothes from the hall closet so we can add them to the sale."

T.J. heads inside to grab the clothes. Momma has him hang them on the old clothesline beside the garage. Then she covers them with an old quilt.

"There's no chance of rain in the weather forecast," Daddy says.

"That's good," Momma says. "We don't want to have a rainy day sale. That would be just awful!"

My friends and I make the signs on white poster board squares. On each sign, we write GARAGE SALE in capital letters. Then we write my address in our best handwriting. Under that, we put the hours, 8 a.m. to 5 p.m.

I make little doggie faces and bones along the edges of my sign.

We make cupcake posters, too. Our posters are so cute. They have pink cupcakes with glitter on them and all the names and prices of the cupcakes.

T.J. walks by with his old sports gear for the sale. He tells us we should work more and talk less.

He just says that because he doesn't have anyone to talk to but Ugly Brother, who is following him around like a caboose on a choo-choo train.

Next, my friends and I use the pink stickers I picked out to make price tags. Lucy and I write the prices down, while Cara and Paula help Momma set things up on the tables.

Ugly Brother gets tired of helping T.J. and wanders over to me. I ask, "Are you goin' to help us now?"

He barks, "Ruff, ruff."

I give him a sheet of stickers to take to Momma. "Don't drool on these," I warn him. He gets one stuck on his nose. I laugh, pluck the sticker off, and tell him, "You're worth more than fifty cents!"

T.J. has a stack of video games he doesn't play anymore. "These are only worth fifty cents," he says. Paula starts putting the stickers on them right away.

"Stop!" I shout. "We should mark them a dollar. Remember, we're tryin' to save the doggies."

Paula says, "Right. I need some dollar stickers."

Daddy is selling his old stamp collection, some books, and some black boots with spurs on the backs. Momma thinks we can get a lot of money for the stamps and the boots. Books will only get fifty cents, but we put ten dollars on the boots.

I price my lemon cupcake cutie doll for five dollars. Momma marks the baby clothes, winter coats, Christmas ornaments, and my stuffed animals.

Ugly Brother wants to bring something to put in the sale, too! It's an ice-cream-cone chew toy, but he chewed the bottom right off and now it looks like a cupcake.

"Don't hurt his feelings," Lucy says. "Put it in the sale anyway."

I put twenty-five cents on it, but seeing that dog toy makes me think of that poor little girl dog at the shelter. I tell my friends all about Tess the dog. Then I add, "I sure hope she gets a family."

"Who do we know that needs a dog?" Paula asks.

Lucy shouts, "Miss Clarabelle!"

"That's right!" I say. "She said she gets lonely in her house. Tess would be perfect!"

Daddy always says that seeing is believing. If I bring Miss Clarabelle to the Puppy Place, seeing Tess will make her want to take that doggie home and keep her forever.

But that will have to wait until after the sale. Tonight, Momma's ordering us some pizza, and then we need to get lots of rest before the big day. All we have to do is wait until tomorrow. Hurry up, morning!

Chapter Nine
Garage Sale Heaven

The next morning, Momma wakes me up while it's still dark outside. Time to get my cupcakes ready!

After lining the cupcakes up on trays and piling them on stands, I carefully cover them with plastic wrap. I twirl it around and around so they will stay fresh.

Then I grab my little pencil bag with change in it, a notepad to write my sales on, and some brown paper lunch sacks to put the cupcakes in.

I set up right in front of the garage where everyone can see me. Kylie Jean Cupcakes is open for business!

People begin to arrive just as the sun comes up! Those garage sale customers are serious. Momma and Daddy don't even get any coffee. We are busy!

Soon, Miss Clarabelle comes over. "I just love Christmas decorations," she remarks, digging through a box.

I know I need to ask her about going to the Puppy Place. "Are you busy tomorrow after church?" I ask. "Because I want you to meet someone."

"Why, I'd love to meet a friend of yours," she tells me, smiling. "I'll see you right after church, then."

"Do you want to buy one of these scrumptious strawberry cupcakes?" I ask, holding up a cupcake.

She smiles again and says, "How can I refuse? They sound wonderful."

She pays me with a five-dollar bill. When I try to give her change back, she tells me I can keep it. Yay! I have some extra money for the puppies!

More of our neighbors and friends come to our sale. Daddy tells them we're donating the money we make to keep the dog shelter open. A lot of people tell us to keep the change for the dogs.

Every time someone walks up, I say, "Delicious cupcakes for sale! Get your cupcakes!"

Granny and Pappy arrive with donuts, coffee, and Lucy. They buy a dozen of my cupcakes! Ka-ching, ka-ching!

Then Lucy comes to help. Together we shout, "Delicious cupcakes for sale! Get your cupcakes here!"

I am pretty excited when my bus driver, Mr. Jim, comes by. He looks down at my table and says, "I'll take a dozen cupcakes. Did your momma help you bake them?"

"Yes, sir," I say, "and she is the best baker in Texas."

"They sure do look tasty," he says. "I don't think I can wait to eat one, so I'll have one right now." He chooses a red velvet cupcake and finishes it in two bites!

Mr. Jim looks around for a while and buys some of Daddy's old tools.

I think I am in garage sale heaven, but after lunchtime, it slows down. Lucy and I stand by the street with a cupcake sale sign, ready to wave at any cars that pass by. We don't see any.

At three o'clock, a lot of customers start coming again. I think these people are hoping to get a deal. Granny says that people like to offer less and they figure at the end of the sale you might just take less.

Cole, my friend from across the street, wanders over. He says, "Hey, y'all."

"Want to buy a cupcake?" I ask.

Cole looks at the cupcakes on my table. "Sure," he says. "But don't give me one with a dog bone on it."

There are only a few cupcakes on my table. There are a few dog cupcakes left, but every dog who tried them ate them right up. I'm glad I made them!

When five o'clock finally comes, we close the sale. It's time to clean up, but we're all tired. Garage sale days are long days!

There's still work to do. Daddy and T.J. put the leftover sale stuff in the back of the truck to go to the Goodwill store. Momma counts the money. Lucy and I help. We roll the coins.

Finally, Momma announces, "We made two hundred and twenty dollars and twenty-five cents for the Puppy Place!"

Lucy and I jump around and do a happy dance.

"Pretty good for a bunch of old stuff we didn't need anyway," Daddy says, smiling. "Kylie Jean can take a check over to the Puppy Place tomorrow after church."

"I hope it's enough to keep the shelter open until we can get more donations," Momma says. Then she looks at me. "We should figure out your profit," she says. When she sees my confused look, she explains, "A profit is how much money you made, not including the money you spent on supplies."

"How much did you spend at the Piggly Wiggly?" Daddy asks.

Momma thinks. "About twenty dollars, I think," she says.

"And how much did you make at the sale?" Daddy asks me.

"I sold sixty-seven cupcakes!" I say proudly.

Daddy announces, "You made a forty-seven-dollar profit."

I smile. "That's a lot of money to bring to the doggie shelter," I say.

Ugly Brother really likes the idea. He barks, "Ruff, ruff!"

I'm tired from working hard all day, but my job isn't over. Now it's time to find a home for Tess.

Chapter Ten
Puppy Love

On Sunday afternoon, Miss Clarabelle comes over after church. "Who did you want me to meet, Kylie Jean?" she asks. "Is he or she here?"

"No," I tell her. "We have to go to the Puppy Place. I want you to meet my friend Mr. Jay."

"Oh, how nice," Miss Clarabelle says.

"Besides, I have to take the check and the doggie cupcakes to the shelter," I add. I don't tell her that secretly, I'm hoping she'll find a new puppy friend!

Ms. Clarabelle drives us over in her big white Cadillac. When we get there, the sign on the door says "open," so we go right in.

Mr. Jay looks up when we walk in. He says, "Well, hello, Miss Kylie Jean. How is our favorite patron today?"

I am puzzled. Frowning, I ask, "Can you please tell me what a patron is so I can answer your question?"

Mr. Jay laughs his big laugh. "A patron is a supporter," he says. "Someone who helps out. Just like you, helping out the Puppy Place."

"Oh!" I say. "Well, okay, I'm just fine and dandy. I brought my friend. We have something to give you, too."

Miss Clarabelle nudges me. "Please introduce me to your friend," she says quietly.

"Mr. Jay," I say, "This is my dear friend Miss Clarabelle."

"Pleased to meet you, ma'am," Mr. Jay says. He shakes her hand.

Then I hand him the envelope with the check and he opens it. He looks like a cat that just got a fresh fish dinner. He is so happy. "This is awesome!" he shouts. "With this money, we can stay open a little longer. Thank you so much, Kylie Jean."

"You're welcome," I say. "We're not givin' up, either. I want to raise some more money for you."

"That would be wonderful," Mr. Jay says.

Then I hear a quiet bark from the back room. That reminds me of the other reason we're here!

"Come on, Miss Clarabelle!" I say, grabbing her hand.

The puppies are all so cute. Miss Clarabelle and I stop at each cage. I tell her about each dog, and then we give them a doggie cupcake. They love them and eat them right up.

I save Tess's cage for last. When we get to her, she has a pink bow tied around her neck and looks so adorable. Mr. Jay lets her come out to play. Right away, the sweet little doggie gives Miss Clarabelle some sweet doggie kisses.

Miss Clarabelle sighs. "This is the prettiest, sweetest dog I've ever seen," she says.

I think it's love at first sight! "Her name is Tess," I tell her. "Short for Countess. I am so worried that Mr. Jay might not be able to find a home for her."

"That's true," Mr. Jay says. "She's the sweetest dog, but no one seems to want an older dog. Everyone just wants the puppies."

I can tell Miss Clarabelle is concerned. I say, "What if nobody wants her? Thinkin' about that makes me sadder than a hen without a chick."

Miss Clarabelle thinks for a minute. "You know," she says, "I get a little lonely in my big old house. If you could help me walk her sometimes, Kylie Jean, I think Tess could come and live with me."

I shout, "Hooray!"

Mr. Jay smiles. "You can fill out the adoption papers right now and take her home today," he says.

As soon as we're back at Miss Clarabelle's house, we sit on the front porch and watch Tess play in the yard. Ugly Brother knows I'm back, and he wants to see what's going on. He comes over. Right away, they start playing, and Ugly Brother licks Tess's ear.

I think that both Ugly Brother and Miss Clarabelle are falling in love with Tess!

I say, "Miss Clarabelle, I am so happy you decided to be Tess's new family. Now I can visit her all the time." Ugly Brother is happy, too. He comes over and licks Miss Clarabelle's hand.

"Are you trying to say thank you?" I ask.

Both of the doggies bark.

Ugly Brother barks, "Ruff, ruff!"

Tess barks, "Woof, woof!"

Two barks means yes!

Miss Clarabelle just pats Ugly Brother on the head. "You're welcome," she says.

The doggies sit on the steps together. They are so cute! Looking at them, I decide it must be puppy love!

Chapter Eleven
Out of Business

On Sunday night, our whole family is sitting at the supper table. The kitchen smells good, like chicken noodle soup.

Momma always makes soup when she is busy because it's easy. You put all of the ingredients in the pot and it cooks by itself.

Daddy asks, "Kylie Jean, when is your next sale going to be?"

"I'm all out of stuff to sell, but I can ask my friends," T.J. says.

"Don't worry," I say. "Granny and Pappy offered to have a sale so I can sell cupcakes."

Momma asks, "Are you ready to bake all of those cupcakes again? You still have a lot of them left over."

I reply, "Yup! Baking is fun."

Then Momma asks, "Guess what's for dessert?"

You guessed it — leftover cupcakes! They are sitting all over the kitchen counter like sweet little red and pink polka dots. I've had so many cupcakes that they don't even look good anymore. Maybe I don't want to be in the cupcake business after all.

Looking at all those leftover cupcakes, an idea hits me like sprinkles on a cupcake!

"How about a going-out-of-business sale?" I say.

Ugly Brother barks twice. That means yes!

And then we each eat one more cupcake.

Marci Bales Peschke was born in Indiana, grew up in Florida, and now lives in Texas with her husband, two children, and a feisty black-and-white cat named Phoebe. She loves reading and watching movies.

When **Tuesday Mourning** was a little girl, she knew she wanted to be an artist when she grew up. Now, she is an illustrator who lives in South Pasadena, CA. She especially loves illustrating books for kids and teenagers. When she isn't illustrating, Tuesday loves spending time with her husband, who is an actor, and their two sons.

Glossary

business (BIZ-niss)—a company that sells things

donate (DOH-nate)—to give something as a present

etiquette (ET-uh-ket)—rules of polite behavior

ingredients (in-GREE-dee-uhnts)—items that something is made from

invest (in-VEST)—to spend money on something in hopes that you will get more money back

loan (LOHN)—something borrowed

permission (pur-MISH-uhn)—if you give permission for something, you say you will allow it to happen

profit (PROF-it)—the amount of money left after all of the costs of running a business are subtracted from earnings

shelter (SHEL-tur)—a place where animals that are not wanted can stay until they are adopted

Talk!

1. Kylie Jean donated all of her profits to the animal shelter. What would you have done with the money?

2. Kylie Jean's whole family worked together to have the garage sale. What other things could they have done to raise money?

3. What do you think happens after this story ends? Talk about it!

Be Creative!

1. Kylie Jean's goal is to be a beauty queen.
   What's your number-one dream?

2. Who is your favorite character in this story?
   Draw a picture of that person. Then write a list of
   five things you know about them.

3. Create your own perfect cupcake! What's in it?
   What does it look like? What does it taste like?
   Draw a picture!

This is the perfect treat for any cupcake queen!
Just make sure to ask a grown-up for help.

Love, Kylie Jean

From Momma's Kitchen

PRINCESS CUPCAKES

YOU NEED:

1 box of your favorite cake mix (any flavor)

1 can of your favorite flavor frosting (not white)

sprinkles, colored sugar — whatever kinds you want!

1 tube of decorator's frosting, white color

cupcake liners in your favorite color

a muffin tin

1. Bake cupcakes as directed on your box of cake mix.
   (Make sure a grown-up helps you!)

2. Let cupcakes cool completely. Once the cupcakes cool, frost.

3. Using the decorator's frosting, draw a simple crown on each
   cupcake.

4. Use your sprinkles and colored sugar to fill in the crown.

Yum, yum!

THE FUN DOESN'T STOP HERE!

Discover more at www.capstonekids.com

♥ Videos & Contests
❀ Games & Puzzles
♥ Friends & Favorites
❀ Authors & Illustrators

Find cool websites and more books like this one at www.facthound.com. Just type in the Book ID: 9781404875807 and you're ready to go!